C. Samuel

A Second Chance

C. Samuel

A Second Chance

Atlanta, GA

ISBN: 978-1-7355058-0-0 (paperback)
ISBN: 978-1-7355058-1-7 (ebook)

Library of Congress Control Number: 2020915627

Edited by Abigail Walker, Allwrite Communications Inc.

Printed in the United States

Contents

1

N o, No! Stop, Tony. Please Stop! I won't disappoint you again. Please stop hitting me!"

"Bitch, didn't I tell you to make sure the dishwasher was full before you turned it on? Wash the motherfucking dishes if it's not full. I am tired of your bullshit."

"You need to just get rid of her useless ass, Son," Debra says as she kicks Tracey in the leg.

"You're right, Ma."

Tony slaps her once more as Tracey pulls herself up and wipes the blood from her mouth.

He then grabs her by the throat and says, "I should just kill you right here and now."

He reaches for his gun in his waistband and pulls the hammer back. The gun clicks. Tony pulls the trigger.

She shuts her eyes tight and screams.

Waking up suddenly in a cold sweat, she looks around and touches her face to make sure it was just a dream. She runs to the bathroom and looks at herself in the mirror. Beads of sweat run down her face. Her heart races, and she shakes like an addict needing a fix.

"It… it was just a dream," she whispers. She takes a few deep breaths to try and calm herself down.

It felt so real, just like all the other times.

For five years, she has been living this nightmare and finally mustered up the strength to leave her abusive husband. After she washes her face, she reaches for a sleep aid to help her calm her nerves.

She pours a couple of sleeping pills into her hands and gets ready to take them with some water, when she looks back at the mirror. She can still envision the bruises and black eyes she suffered at the hands of her husband.

"I'll take a few more; I need to shake this feeling," she says to herself.

As she is about to take the pills, she then looks up in the mirror to her right and sees her son standing there with tears rolling down his cheeks.

"Mommy, please don't cry,"

Tracey looks at her son and pours the pills down the sink. She reaches over and hugs her son.

"We are going to be okay. He can't hurt us anymore. I love you and Charisse so much, and I promise you that will never change."

"I love you, Mommy."

"I love you too, Jay Jay."

Tracey knows that she has to testify against her soon-to-be ex-husband in the morning. She tucks her son back into his bed and kisses him goodnight as she turns on his Spiderman night light.

She walks to her bedroom telling herself with every step that she can do this. As she climbs back into the bed, she clutches her pillow tight in her arms and drifts off to sleep.

The next morning, Tracey takes Jason to school and drops Charisse off at the day care. She heads back home to get dressed before heading to the courthouse. Her doorbell rings. It's her future ex-mother-in-law Debra Parker at the door.

"Who is it?"

"It's Debra, hoe. Now open the damn door."

"What the hell does she want," she says under her breath. "Just a minute. I just got out of the shower."

Tracey runs to get her cell phone and dials 911.

"I need the police to 9104 Shadow Road. There is a woman at my door harassing me."

"We will send a car right away."

Tracey runs to the bathroom to get her bathrobe and walks to the front door slowly. She takes a deep breath and unlocks the door, but she leaves the screen door locked.

"What can I do for you?"

Debra tries to come in but realizes it's still locked.

"Aren't you going to let me in, dear?"

"No, I am getting ready for court, and I don't have time for your nonsense. What do you want? I've had enough drama from you and your son."

Debra's smile fads fast.

"Listen up, bitch. You need to come clean about how you pushed my son into the situation he is in now. You need to tell the whole truth about your role."

"Look, I am sick and tired of you and your son. He's beat me and terrorized me, which has left a lasting effect on my children—the grandchildren who you barely acknowledge."

Debra reaches for the door to open it again as she says, "Look, bitch. I don't give a fuck about them kids. I'm not sure if they are my sons' anyway. You know you're nothing but a town hoe. Hell, you've been

3

with enough men in this town. Now, either you come clean today, or I'm going to come clean you tomorrow. Your choice."

She flashes a small gun that is in her purse for Tracey to see.

At the same time, a horn blows from the street, and she immediately looks in that direction.

Tracey's eyes grow wide as soon as sees the gun, and she slams the door really fast and moves away from it before she can use it on her.

"Dumb bitch, I don't know what the hell my son saw in that trick."

Debra walks fast towards the car that blew the horn. She can hear the police sirens getting louder. She gets into the car, and they drive off before the police arrive.

Once the police show up, Tracey explains what happened. They take her statement and promise to escort her to the courthouse.

2

6 Weeks Later

Mr. Parker, a jury of your peers have found you guilty of possession with intent to sell in the 2nd degree, assault in 2nd degree and spousal battery in the 1st degree. Do you have a statement to the court before sentencing?"

"No, Your Honor. Just know that I am innocent."

"In that case, this court sentences you to the following: possession with intent to sell in the 2nd degree—eight years, assault in the 2nd degree—seven years and spousal battery in the 1st degree—five years. These sentences are to run consecutively for a total of 20 years in a facility to be determined by the Department of Corrections of the State of New York. Court is adjourned."

The police immediately place handcuffs on to Tony as he turns to look at his mother who has tears in her eyes. Debra reaches over the bannister to hug her son. Immediately, they both turn their heads and look at Tracey as she leaves the courtroom.

"This is your fault, you lying hoe. You are not going to get away with your lies. She needs to be arrested."

Debra hugs Tony once more as he is led by the officers out of the courtroom to be led to jail.

Tracey is escorted out by an officer and held with another officer in the waiting room until things calm down. She is still shaking from everything.

Debra makes a bee line out of the courtroom yelling Tracey's name the whole time. "Where is that lying bitch? I know she is around here somewhere."

"Miss, you need to calm down," the court officer says to her.

"Get the hell out of my way. I know she is in there. Come on out, bitch."

Debra is able to kick the door one time before the officer moves her back.

Tracey hears Debra's voice and begins to cry.

"Ma'am, this is your last warning. Leave now before I place you under arrest. You can't go in this room."

"Fuck you," Debra says to the officer as she turns and walks away. "I'll get that bitch another way."

The officer shakes his head as he enters the waiting room to check on Tracey.

After the defense files an appeal on the guilty verdict, the prosecution and defense file into a courtroom in Manhattan. The appellate judges hear the evidence and rule against the motion.

Three weeks later, a letter is sent with no return address to the home of Tracey Parker. Inside, there is a picture of a battered and bruised Tracey and a note attached. The note said, "Hey, bitch. It's a shame I won't do this to you for a while, but enjoy the memories of all the times I would fuck and beat you until I got tired.

For testifying against me, I am going to get even with you if it's the last thing I do. You betrayed our vows together for better or for worse. Just wait and see. You won't see it coming. Love you always, Tony."

Tracey immediately rips the letter up and throws it into the trash.

The next day, as Tracey leaves to take Jason to school and Charisse to the sitter, she thinks she sees someone around the back of her house, but she dismisses it as a neighbor. As she closes the door to her car, currently parked on the street, she hears the sound of a window being broken. As she starts to open the door to investigate, an explosion happens in her kitchen. There is glass everywhere. The fire and smoke begin to rise into the air. The kids begin to scream.

A car door slams on the next block, and a vehicle races away from the scene. Neighbors begin to run over to try and assist.

The police and the fire department are called to investigate. Everything in the home is destroyed. The Fire Department determines the cause to be a pipe bomb that was thrown into the kitchen. Tracey immediately knows that Tony was behind it.

Her cell phone rings from a blocked number, and she hears a muffled, female voice on the other end as it laughs uncontrollably.

"Where do I go from here?" she asks herself. She hugs her kids tight and begins to sob.

3

3 Years Later

Tracey, can you please work late tonight? We need to work on the Barksdale account," Mr. James, her boss, asks.

"Sure," Tracey answers with a less than enthusiastic smile. "Oh well. I better call Mike."

Tracey and Mike have been married for two years. This is his second marriage as well. Mike lost his wife of 8 years to a sudden stroke, due to hypertension. He was left to raise their 2 children Ashley, who is now 7, and Tommy, who is now 3, alone. Tracey's son, Jason is now 9 and Charrise is now 4.

"Hello."

"Hey, handsome. I am going to be home late. I was just asked to work late tonight."

"No problem, love. I got it covered, but what time do you think you will be home?"

"I think about 9."

"Ok, don't worry. The kids and I will be fine."

"I love you so much. I do not deserve you. Bye, handsome."

"Bye, sexy. Love you too."

Mike looks at his watch and realizes its 4 p.m. He says to his self, "Oops, I need to get the kids from the daycare center."

Mike parks his car in the parking lot and proceeds into the lobby to sign the kids out. "Hi, Mrs. Allen," he says and walks into the toddler room of Royal Childcare.

"How are you, Mr. Cohen?" Mrs. Allen asks. The sky blue clouds painted on the walls momentarily distracts Mike from Mrs. Allen's question.

When the kids see him, they run, yelling, "Daddy!"

Mike hugs them both, one in each arm. "Get your things. We have to go."

"Is Tracey working late again?" Before he could answer, she adds, "You two seem to have a great marriage by the way you guys work together. I wish more people your age would work as well as you two do."

Mike was about to say something smart but catches himself. "Thanks, we really do. I am so glad to have her as my wife. I never thought I would ever find true love again after Debbie passed away. God truly sent her just for me."

Mike thinks about Debbie's last words to him before she slipped back into a coma: "Take care of our babies. I love you."

"Ready?" Mike says to the kids, and they nod their heads.

"Say goodbye to Mrs. Allen," he says.

"Bye, Mrs. Allen," they yell as they walk out the door.

Mike then goes to pick up Jason and Ashley from the library. He drives up to the find them waiting outside to meet him.

"Hey, Dad," they both say at the same time as they climb in the SUV.

"Where's Mommy?" Ashley asks.

"She is working late tonight."

"I need help with my math," says Jason.

"We'll look at it at home, Son. Okay?"

"Cool."

They drive up to their home, a nice, two-story Victorian home in Roslyn, New York, which they purchased when they got married.

"Everybody out," Mike calls.

As they go inside, each child walks into the house and goes their separate ways. Ashley and Cherise go to their room to change their clothes. Jason goes to the bathroom and Tommy goes to watch television. He turns on Rugrats and begins to sing the theme song. Mike heads for the kitchen to start making dinner for the kids. He fixes fried chicken and green beans. Meanwhile, the older kids start their homework. Mike checks in on them as the phone rings.

"Hello," answers Mike.

"Hey, handsome. How's it going?"

"Everything is going great. Hold on, the kids want to talk to you."

"Hey, Mommy."

"Hi, kids."

"Are you being good for Daddy?"

"Yes."

"Ok, I will see you all when I get home. I love you."

"Hey," Mike says as he returns to the line. "Does 9 o'clock still look good?"

"Yes. What's for dinner? Or should I bring something home for us?"

"Nope. I have it covered."

"I love you."

"Love you more," he replies as he hangs up the phone.

Mike finishes dinner and begins to assemble the plates for the kids. Mike yells, "Dinner is ready."

All the kids make their way into the kitchen and sit down.

"This is good," says Ashley as she eats. All the kids nod their heads in agreement.

"Thanks."

As the kids finish dinner, they make their way into the den to start watching television. Mike starts to help Jason with his math homework.

"Here is the problem," his son says as they work together.

"Thanks for the help, Dad," Jason says.

"No problem, Son."

Jason joins his brother and sisters in the den to watch their show. In the meantime, Mike starts to cook for Tracey.

"Let's see," he says to himself. "Lobster, baked potato, and green beans."

Mike then checks on the kids and then starts to prepare the lobster and the salad.

At 8 p.m., Mike calls, "Bedtime!"

The kids get on their feet and easily go up to bed. Mike tucks them all in as dinner begins to come together. He closes the door to their room and begins to change his clothes.

Mike and Tracey always dedicate one night a week for "quality time." They never have a set time, and one of them always takes the initiative.

At 8:50 p.m., after dinner is cooked and sits simmering on the stove, Mike gives a final check on the kids. As he suspected, everyone is sound asleep. Mike goes downstairs to the den and proceeds to play Tracey's favorite slow jams on the CD player. He dims the lights and begins to set the mood for the evening.

"The red wine is set, the dinner is simmering, the lights are dim and the music is on. What is missing?" he says softly. "I got it."

He makes his way to the bathroom, lights the scented candles and runs the bath water for his tired wife.

"Good night, Tracey," says Jill, one of her co-workers.

"Good night, Jill."

"I'm so tired," she sighs. "I hope I'm going to sleep good tonight."

As she makes the 15-minute drive home, she notices the lights are dim at her house.

"I wonder if he is asleep," she says to herself.

She gets out of her Toyota Camry and walks to the front door. As she walks in the door, the smell of the dinner hits her immediately. She then hears the faint sound of "Anytime, Anyplace" coming from the CD player. She then begins to perk up and smile.

"What is he up to?" she says to herself.

She then makes her way to the bathroom where she finds the Jacuzzi jets flowing in the tub. She smells the scented candles and sees a change of clothes hanging up for her. She has a big smile on her face.

"Wow," she says softly to herself. "He did this for me."

A tear begins to form in her left eye. Tracey thinks back to her previous disaster of a marriage before Mike. She thinks about the beatings, the verbal abuse, the trips to the hospital and the different shades of make-up she purchased to hide the bruises. Tony was a controlling, manipulating bully.

She places her purse on the table as Mike appears, smiling. He is wearing pajama pants that show off his muscular frame and immediately make her forget her long day. As he walks near her, she begins to smell his cologne. He greets her with a special hug and soft kiss. Their height is perfect for each other. He is 5'9" with a shaved head and trimmed moustache. He has muscular arms and legs, and Tracey is always turned on when she sees his muscles. She is 5'4" with 42DD breasts, chocolate brown skin, wavy, jet-black hair and a firm body all over.

"Go take your bath. Dinner is ready when you are."

As he turns to leave, she grabs his arm and says to him, "Where are you going? This tub was made for two."

They proceed to kiss and help each other undress. He helps her into the tub. Mike stops for a second.

"Do you have any idea how gorgeous you are?"

As Mike begins to slide inside of his wife, Tracey throws her head back while her arms are still wrapped around Mike's neck. The water begins to thrash violently from the waves they are producing. Mike tells her he is ready to climax.

"Fill me now," moaned Tracey. "I am so ready."

Mike obliged her, staring deeply in her eyes.

They climax together, and in an instant, the water begins to calm down. They proceed to get out of the tub and dry each other off. Tracey proceeds to put on a seductive nightgown with a robe. Mike puts on the pajama pants that she likes and his robe.

"This is not over," she says to him in a firm voice.

Mike then leads her to the kitchen to eat dinner. Tracey sits down with a big smile on her face. Mike begins to serve the dinner he carefully prepared. Tracey cannot believe her eyes.

"Are you trying to make me fat?" she asks her husband.

"Don't worry, love. We will work it off together."

"Will we?" she asks with a coy expression.

Mike had come to know that look very well. It was one of many reasons he fell for her so hard, so fast after his first marriage. Those eyes could command a room without saying a word. He thought back to the first day they met.

"What else can possibly go wrong?" Mike thought to himself as he hurriedly exited the now empty airport van. "It's almost 9 p.m. How the hell is that possible when I made it into John Wayne Airport at 7p.m. and the Marriott is a mere 10 minutes away?"

He asked himself the question without really wanting to know the answer, particularly since he finally made it to the hotel. With his mind racing forward now, he allowed himself to indulge in thought. All the therapeutic satisfaction he needed right now was his for the taking during this week long "business trip."

He didn't have to think about anything, not the sudden passing of his wife, the babies or anyone else. All he had to do was stay awake during the day-long business presentations and fill his evenings with all the spoils this exquisite hotel had to offer.

The driver, after having already placed his luggage on the sidewalk, stood patiently before Mike with wide eyes and a wider grin, just waiting.

"You do realize you wouldn't be any more obvious if you went ahead and held your hand out, don't you?" Mike said to him.

"Sir, I know you're upset about the transport delay, but you were the first one to enter the van. First in, last out."

Before he could finish his explanation for taking the scenic route, he realized Mike was already handing him $5.

"Thank you, sir. Thank you kindly for your generosity, and be sure to make reservations a day in advance for your transport back to the airport."

Ironically, he now carried Mike's luggage all the way into the hotel now. Mike walked behind him, nonchalant to his almost sincere patronage and barely listening.

"Thanks again, Mr. Cohen, and enjoy your trip," the driver said, smiling while making his exit.

Only now did Mike realize there were 4 people ahead of him, waiting to be checked in. That's not too bad. He would just get his Corporate AMEX along with his confirmation number out and have them ready. At least that would expedite the process when it was his turn.

"In just a few minutes, I can get out of this suit and relax," Mike whispered to himself. He felt his back pocket. "Hmm. That's odd. It's empty."

He digs all the way down into his pocket, which was void of his wallet but not lint.

"What the hell," he said before looking back toward the doors where he was relieved to see his briefcase still on the sidewalk where he left it. "Get a grip, man. In just a few minutes, you can settle down, unwind and chill."

The woman, who bent down to pick up his briefcase before he could get to it, interrupted his thoughts. He watched her, as she appeared to be examining it, perhaps for I.D.

"Excuse me. That's my briefcase. May I have it please?" Mike said to the woman in a shaky voice.

Mike shifted with uneasiness as she gazed at him with apparent doubt. Before saying a word, she twisted, tugged at her skirt and re-adjusted it after bending over.

"And just how am I supposed to know that? I think I'll go ahead and take it inside to the reservations desk."

Before walking away, she shot him that expression, once again; her eyes were wide open but one appeared to be slightly wider than the other and that eye's brow rose. Yes, it was definitely a look of suspicion. Mike, now standing outside alone without his briefcase, couldn't figure out why he was so completely confused. Was it because this strange female actually had the nerve to carry his briefcase away, with all of her own luggage in tow? Was it because he now realized that he lost his place in line as #5, or was it something else, something more? Why on earth did that brazen expression on her face excite him?

"Excuse me. I realize there is a line here, but someone left a briefcase just outside your hotel. I believe it may belong to someone staying here perhaps," the young lady said as she glanced in Mike's direction.

"Thank you," she continued as she went to the back of the line.

Mike caught up to her and said, "Miss, I told you that was my briefcase."

"Is that right?"

"Yes."

"Well, if it's your briefcase as you claim, you will have ID, won't you?"

"Yes, as a matter of fact, I do."

"Good, let's see it."

"It's...It's..."

"Yes? It's...what?" she asks slightly raising her voice.

Mike's lack of response spawned her final remark. "Uh huh. I didn't think so."

He stood there in disbelief. He thought, "This woman is challenging me about my own property, and the nerve of her to have on my favorite perfume."

She was wearing Sensitive Spark, a scent he had come to love from a college sweetheart. He continued to watch the woman who now captured his attention.

Ignoring Mike, she speaks to the hotel clerk. "Yes, good evening. My name is Tracey Parker. I'm with James & Associates Advertising Group. I have a reservation."

Mike continued to watch her, not worried about the incident with his briefcase. He was, however, still unnerved by the way she looked at him and wondered to himself, just what if. Standing there behind her, he couldn't help but notice her firm ass. He willed himself to look away and to think of something else.

"Your briefcase, sir?" the counter service rep broke his line of thought.

"I'm sorry. What did you say?"

"Ms. Parker said this may be your briefcase."

"Oh, Yes," Mike says before clearing his throat. "Yes, it is. Thank you."

"You will have to produce your ID before we can release the briefcase. You do realize that, don't you?"

"This is unbelievable. This is just not my day."

Just then, he noticed her, Ms. Parker. She was still standing there watching, obviously enjoying the bad ordeal that she created.

"Ma'am, my name is Michael Cohen," he said to the hotel clerk. "My confirmation number is J76227. I have a reservation for a suite for the next 4 nights. I am representing a prospective client for 6 nationally known advertising agencies competing for our business this week. I am scheduled to speak first thing in the morning. Now you can either hand me my briefcase, or we can call your boss and get this whole matter worked out another way."

Completely frazzled, the hotel receptionist apologized profusely and handed Mike his briefcase.

Before he walked away, he noticed his little audience, and the fact that he still had her undivided attention despite her demeanor was different.

"Ms. Parker, was it?" Mike asked.

"Yes. Tracey Parker."

"Ms. Parker, of James and Associates, I believe you are on the presentation panel."

"Yes...yes I am."

Mike watched her with that same expression on her face that incited him to several emotions within just a few minutes. Only now, she was not suspicious, nor was she sarcastic. She was shy. He continued to study her now, staring even, at those eyes. That one brow still lifted slightly, and those lips slightly glossed and pouted.

"You are ready to present, aren't you, Ms. Parker?" Mike asked as he started to walk toward the elevators.

"Look, Mr. Cohen. I'm sorry about this whole situation, but I did do the right thing. I just hope you won't hold it against me or my agency."

Thinking about what she said, he paused and sighed, smelling her perfume again. It was apparent that he was impressed by her professionalism, perhaps even by something else.

"I'll see you in the morning. Good night, Ms. Parker," Mike said as he stepped into the elevator.

He turned around to face the elevator doors and noticed Tracey still standing there. For the first time this evening, with eye contact between them, a connection was established. It was absolutely almost like fate.

"Will we?" Tracey asks again, rousing Mike from his reminiscing. Without answering her, he watches her busily eat her lobster. Mike comes around the table and kneels down beside her.

"What are you doing, handsome?"

"You dripped, love."

He then grabs her right hand, brings her forefinger to his lips and slowly sucks off the remnants of the butter sauce. After they finish dinner, they make their way into the den where the CD player is set to specific selections. Tracey and Mike lie on the couch, relax and listen to the music. Tracey tells Mike about her day and declares that she needs a massage. Mike leads her to the bedroom and proceeds to undress her for a full body rubbing. He had already set up a bottle of red wine and strawberries.

"Oh baby. My favorite! Have I told you how deep in love I am with you, and goodness, how much I appreciate you?"

"Mike, I really did not think I would ever be able to love again after what he did to me."

His left hand comes to her mouth and to those lips and hushes her.

"That was the past."

His right hand reaches behind her neck to slowly pull her body and her mouth forward to his. The kiss is gentle; the lightest brush of his lips is endearing to her and completely erotic. He touches his lips to hers again but this time with no gentleness. It is long and deep, and Tracey feels as though she had melted. Before long, she has forgotten about the massage she asked for and all the stress of the day and focuses on how wonderful and thorough her handsome husband is for kissing and caressing her. His hands move to her back to push her closer, and she can feel him trembling. She gets the feeling that he was as excited as she was, and it is such a flattering feeling to be longed for so much.

C. Samuel

His hands move all over her, through her hair, along her throat and around her breasts.

"Oh...yes!" Mike exclaims.

Tracey then falls onto Mike as they embrace from such a passionate and intense love making manifestation of their love for each other. They then proceed to fall asleep in each other's arms. As they share one final kiss for the evening, Tracey and Mike fall asleep in each other's arms.

4

About an hour later, Tracey jumps up in a cold sweat.

"No!" she yells as she remembers her first marriage, one she is desperate to forget. Mike wakes up sensing something is wrong with his wife.

"You had another nightmare again?"

"Yeah."

Mike turns on the lights. He immediately wipes the tears from her eyes as they start to well up.

"Do you want to talk about it? Or was it the same as the others?"

"The same as before," she says shaking and in scared tone. "I can still feel him hitting me and kicking me while he has that sick smirk on his face."

"Mike, do you remember when we first met? I was trying to be a bitch on purpose. I was attracted to you, but I was a bit afraid. That's why I acted the way I did. He stole a lot of my confidence, but it seems like almost instantly you helped me get it back."

Mike proceeds to give her a comforting hug and tells her, "He can never hurt you again."

Tracey nods her head in agreement to her husband. She remembers what the judge told him at his sentencing hearing. Tracey's first husband would beat her while high on drugs and alcohol. At his sentencing, the judge sent him away for 20 years. He had already been a two-time offender. She had to testify at his hearing against him. He swore that he would get even with her for leaving him. She and her husband kiss again and fall back asleep.

Later that evening, Tracey wakes up and goes to use the bathroom. As she turns on the light and looks into the mirror, she sees the reflection of her blackened eyes, busted lips and dark bruises on her neck and face. She suddenly gasps and then begins to rub her eyes. She takes a second look in the mirror and sees Tony's image behind her with a sick smile on his face. Tracey takes a breath and quickly looks behind her. She rubs her eyes again and sees her normal face.

"He can't hurt me again."

She thinks about what her pastor and her therapist told her in her many counseling sessions. They say, "her strength comes from God, her children who need her to survive, and the promise that she made to herself to stand up on her own two feet." Then, she thinks about the kids and snaps back to reality.

"I can do this. I can do this," she whispers to herself. "I have a loving husband, a second chance at happiness and a family."

She takes another deep breath and goes back to bed.

5

The next morning, Tony has been summoned for a conference with his attorney to appeal his sentence.

"Mr. Parker, this is going to be a very tough case to overturn on appeal. The main witness, your ex-wife, has the most damaging evidence against you, and I am sure the prosecution will be using her as their star witness again."

"What if she doesn't testify against me in the appeal? How will that change the case?"

"It would alter their presentation tremendously, but what makes you think she won't testify again?"

"Look, just leave that to me. I got that bitch in my back pocket. I am in her head, and she knows it. Plus, I have a back-up plan just in case."

"I need you to deliver this letter to the main post office in the village and make sure you ask for Pebbles. She is expecting it."

Tony just smiles as he is taken back to his cell.

At the same time, Tracey wakes up with a smile on her face. Mike wakes up a minute later and smiles at his pretty wife.

He says to her, "How did you sleep?"

"I feel better just because you were there for me. Thank you, handsome."

Tracey kisses him good morning and heads into the bathroom for a shower. Mike smiles as his naked wife leaves the room. Mike then looks at the time and proceeds to put on his robe and get the kids up for school.

"Time to get up and out of bed!" he exclaims.

One by one, the children move around in their beds and into the bathroom. Charisse and Ashley go in the bathroom first. When they are finished, Tommy and Jason proceed to get ready.

Tracey has made her way to the kitchen to prepare breakfast for the family. The kids all want cold cereal for breakfast. Meanwhile, Mike is in the bathroom getting ready for work.

Ashley and Jason begin to argue like they do every morning.

"Stop it, you two!" she yells at them. Tommy begins to snicker at them for getting in trouble.

"Stop it, Tommy!" Tracey warns him.

It is now 7:30 a.m. Mike comes down the stairs, heads to the table and reads his paper.

"Bye," Jason and Ashley yell as they get their books and leave for the door.

"Have a good day at school," says Tracey.

"Be careful!" says Mike.

Tracey begins to bring Mike his breakfast.

"Breakfast with a smile," he says.

"I smile at other things also, or have you forgotten?"

Mike looks over at their children and back at Tracey as if to say not in front of the kids. Tracey just smiles and sets down Mike's plate in front of him. She then slightly brushes past Mike so he can get a whiff of her perfume since she knows it is his favorite. Charrise and Tommy start to put on their coats to get ready to go to the sitter. Tracey yells to the kids to get their books and head to the door. She walks in to the kitchen to kiss Mike and meets them there. Mike finishes his plate, puts it in the sink and proceeds to head out the door for work.

A couple of hours later, Tracey calls Mike to see how his day is going.

"Hello, this is Mike," he answers.

"Hey, handsome."

"Hey, sexy."

"How is your day going?"

"Better now that I am talking to you."

"Is that right?"

"What are you up to?"

"How about a little lunch?"

"Okay. What do you have a taste for?"

"A little bit of this, a little bit of that and a lot of you."

She laughs discreetly. "I will be home by noon."

"Don't be late, handsome. You might miss something good."

"Trust me. I will be there."

Tracey leaves work at 11:30 a.m. to go to lunch.

"Mr. James, my daughter's school just called. She is sick. Is it okay if I work from home the rest of the day?"

"Yes, Tracey. I hope she feels better. Keep us posted."

Tracey rushes out of the office.

"Hmm," she says to herself. "I need to go by the store. Let me see. I need rose pedals, whip cream, chocolate sauce, strawberries, sparkling cider, scented candles and edible underwear."

By the time she is done shopping, she looks at her watch and notices the time is 11:45. "I need to get home now."

She walks into her home and prepares the atmosphere for Mike's arrival. She begins to set everything up. Meanwhile, Mike pulls up, and of course, he is smiling from ear to ear.

Tracey hears the car door close and begins to make her way up stairs. Mike walks through the door. There are rose pedals on the floor for him to walk on. The room smells so sweet and soft.

"She really knows how to set a mood," he says to his self. "Let me see where these pedals lead."

Mike makes his way upstairs and turns the corner to find Tracey lying on the bed with nothing but an edible bra and panties on. Mike's eyes widen when he sees his wife. Tracey smiles and opens her legs slightly to peak Mike's interest.

"Do you want see how sweet I taste?" she asks him.

"Wow," Mike whispers.

Tracey just smiles, kisses her husband and says, "Just what the doctor ordered."

Mike is a little puzzled but does not say anything to his wife. Just then the door closes downstairs. Mike and Tracey jump out of the bed and rush to get dressed.

"Mom, Dad, anybody home?" Jason yells.

Mike makes his way down and tries to look calm and collected.

"Hey Jay, how was school?" Mike asks.

"School was okay. We had a test in math today. You know that problem we worked on yesterday? It was on the test."

"Oh really? So, you did pretty well?"

"Yes, I think so. Where's mom? I saw her car outside. Is she okay?"

"Yeah, yeah…your mother is okay. She's in the bathroom."

"How is my little man?" Tracey appears with a smile.

Mike breathes a sigh of relief as Tracey joins them.

"Hey, Mom. What are you doing home so early?"

Tracey smiles and tells him that she didn't feel good and needed some relaxation.

"Why don't you start your homework?" Mike says to him.

"Okay."

"Did someone spill some flowers or something?" Jason asks.

Mike begins to turn red as he looks at Tracey and looks at the rose pedals on the carpet. Tracey winks and tells him she has it. Mike proceeds to go downstairs to get something to eat. Tracey proceeds to clean up the rose pedals on the carpet. Mike walks past her and brushes against her.

"And by the way, this isn't over," he says and winks at her.

Tracey just smiles at her husband.

Mike leaves to go get the other kids from the day care.

Meanwhile, Tracey is upstairs when the doorbell rings. Jason answers the door, and it is a certified letter for his mother.

"Who is at the door?" Tracey asks him.

"Are you Tracey Parker?"

"I am Tracey Cohen."

"I have a certified letter for Tracey D. Parker."

Tracey is wondering what is going on. When she looks to see where the letter came from, she has a look of horror on her face.

"Who is the letter from, Mom?" Jason asks her.

"There is no return address."

The letter says, "I am going to get even. Time is ticking…"

"Jason, come inside."

Tracey reads the letter, and she slowly slumps into a chair.

"Mom, what's the matter? What does the letter say?"

"Nothing, baby."

She hugs her son. About 15 minutes later, the car pulls up in the driveway. Mike is home with the other kids. He walks in the door and looks at his wife. He knows something is wrong.

"Hi, Mommy!" The kids say, happy to see her.

"Hi, babies. How was your day?"

Tracey is trying to mask her emotions, but Mike knows his wife too well for that act.

"Kids, give me a minute with your mom, please," Mike says to them.

Mike leads Tracey to another room so that they can talk.

"What's wrong? You have that look upon your face."

"Oh, Mike," Tracey sighs. "Look at this."

"Oh, shit!" Mike's expression changes immediately when he reads it. "When did this come?"

"Right after you left, baby."

Mike looks at the letter again.

"It can't be from him. His ass is locked up. The judge said that he was getting 20 years in prison, so he can't hurt you."

"Baby, Tony has 'friends' that will do his dirty work for him. He just gives the go ahead. I am so scared."

Mike begins to comfort his wife.

"It's going to be ok. I promise you that he will never hurt you."

The doorbell rings at the front door. Tracey immediately jumps in fear. Mike tells her to relax.

"I'll get it."

Mike swings opens the door with force.

"I have a package for Tracey Parker," the courier tells him.

"There is no one here by that name."

As Mike closes the door, the man replies, "Sir, I just delivered a letter to her, but I forgot this package went with it. I know I have the correct address."

"Her name is Cohen now!"

Mike snatches the package from the courier and proceeds to close the door.

"Have a nice day, Mike," he says under his breath.

"What is it, Mike?"

Inside the package are pictures of a battered and beaten Tracey from years ago. Mike is growing more upset by the minute.

"I am putting an end to this."

He rushes back outside to see if the courier is still there, but he has disappeared.

"What are you going do?" Tracey says with a note of concern in her voice.

"This has to stop. If the DA can't do anything about this, then I will. Be back in a few."

Mike hugs Tracey and rushes out the door. About 10 minutes later, the doorbell rings again, and Tracey goes to the door and sees that it is a UPS delivery man.

"Package for Tracey Parker. Sign right here, ma'am."

Tracey signs for the package and takes it from the courier. She walks back inside and opens up the package.

"What the hell," she says.

She looks at a picture of Tony with Charisse in the background at the daycare center. The caption at the bottom reads, "I am this close to getting my baby!"

"I need to call Cheryl."

She grabs her phone and clicks her sister's number with shaking hands.

"Hello?"

"Cheryl, do you know that bastard is taking pictures of Charisse at your center?"

"Tracey? What the hell? What are you talking about? I need you to calm down so I can understand you."

Tracey takes a deep breath and explains the pictures.

Suddenly, it dawns on Cheryl what Tracey is saying.

"Wait, did you say your ex-husband took pictures of Charisse at my center? I am on my way to your house."

Tracey begins to cry. She picks up the phone and calls her mom to vent.

"Hello?" her mother says.

"Hi, Mom. How are you?" she asks as she is trying to hold it together.

"Hi, baby girl. What's wrong? I hear something in your voice."

"Something has happened, Mom, and I am scared. Tony has been sending me these letters and pictures from jail. Now, I think he has escaped from jail. He sent a picture at the center with Charisse."

"Oh my God, Tracey. When did this begin? Did you call your sister? Does Michael know?"

"Cheryl is on her way over. Michael knows about the first picture but not the picture of Charisse," she says as she starts crying again. "He stormed out of the house a few minutes ago."

"I am on my way over with your dad. It's going to be okay, baby."

"Thanks, Mom."

About 30 minutes later, the doorbell rings. Tracey's parents are at the door.

"Grandma, Grandpa!" the kids yell.

"Hey, kids," Todd, Tracey's father, tells them.

"Hi, my babies," Tina, Tracey's mother, adds and reaches out to them. "Jason, you and Ashley take your brother and sister into the other room so we can speak to your mom, please?"

"Okay, Grandma."

As the kids leave the room, Tracey reaches for a tissue.

"Baby girl, what happened? Talk to us."

Before Tracey can open her mouth, Mike walks through the door with Cheryl.

"Hi, Mom. Dad," they both say at the time.

Tracey looks at Cheryl to ask if she mentioned anything to Mike. She shakes her head.

"Hi, Michael. Listen, you are like a natural son to us, and we know that you love Tracey with all you heart. We don't want you to do anything foolish," Tina starts.

"We know that Tony is an idiot, but let the authorities handle this," Todd says. "We don't want anything to happen to you."

"Mike, I need to tell you something, and I need you to remain calm," Tracey continues.

"While you were out, I got another package."

She hands the picture to Mike. Mike looks at the picture and becomes enraged. He looks over at Cheryl and sees red.

"Cheryl, what the hell is going on at that place of yours?"

"Mike, I am just as upset about this as you are. That's my niece also."

"Okay, okay!" Tracey yells. "We are not going to get anything solved by yelling at each other. Mike, I think we should call Chuck and let him investigate this. Tony has escaped from prison, and the cops don't have a clue."

A knock comes from the door. Mike goes to answer it. It is his parents.

"Hello, Son."

"What are you guys doing here?" Mike asks them.

"Tracey's parents called us on the way. Where is Tracey? Are the kids okay?"

Mike lets out a sigh and lets them in.

"C'mon in!"

"Hi, Mary. Milton," Todd says.

They all hug.

"Tracey, how are you? Are you okay? Do the kids know?" Mary asks.

"Calm down. This is why I did not want you guys to know," Mike tells everyone. "Here is the deal. I went to the DA, and they said since the letters don't directly come from Tony, there is nothing that they can do right now. They are going to launch an investigation, but I am not happy with that."

"Son, I understand what you're saying, but what in the world can you do? I'm not putting you down, but you are no match for a major criminal," Milton says.

"Listen! I am not going to do something crazy, but I will protect my wife and family."

He puts his arms around his wife.

"Son," Milton says. "Promise me that you will not involve your crazy cousins in this, please."

"Dad, I won't," Mike says.

"Is it okay for us to come out now?" Jason says.

"I am hungry, Mommy," says Ashley.

"Hey, why don't we all go out to dinner?" Tracey suggests.

"Sounds good to me," Mike says.

As everyone goes out the door, Mike reaches out for Tracey to make sure she is okay.

Tracey just tells her husband, "I love you so much," and then Mike hugs her.

After dinner, they make their way home.

"Good night," Tracey tells her parents as they leave.

"If you're under the age of 10, its time for bed," Mike calls out.

The kids make their way upstairs. Mike and Tracey tuck them in.

"Good night. I love you all," they tell them.

"Mommy, it's going to be okay," Jason tells her.

"Yes, it will, Son," she says and then looks at Mike.

Mike takes his wife by the hand and leads her down the stairs to the living room.

"How are you feeling?"

"Baby, I am nervous. I don't know what he will do next, but I need to know something. What do you have in mind, Michael?"

Mike knows when Tracey calls him that she is concerned or upset.

"Baby, I don't know. I don't know what direction to go. The police are not doing much about this. I was going to ask my cousins to get involved, but that is not the smartest thing to do. I will figure out something."

"No, we will figure something out together."

Mike then goes into the kitchen to get something to drink. Tracey then calls him from the den, "I just need you to hold me."

He picks Tracey up and takes her upstairs to their room. He lays her down on the bed and turns on the television. Mike places his arms around her and just holds her. Eventually, Tracey gets up to go to the bathroom.

Tracey comes back from the bathroom and lies down next to her husband.

"I love you so much Mike. Thank you for being there for me."

All of a sudden, they hear the sound of broken glass downstairs. The noise wakes up Ashley, who begins to cry. Tracey rushes to the girl's room to calm her down. Mike goes into the closet to get his gun. Mike loads the clip and makes his way towards the kitchen.

"The door is still locked," he says, as he turns on the outside light and looks around. The brick that was thrown through the window has a note tied to it.

The note says, "I am going to get even with you, bitch. This is not over."

Mike looks at the note and begins to get heated again. Mike cocks his gun. He then runs outside to look around outside but finds no one.

"This is unbelievable," he says.

"Mike?"

"Stay inside, Tracey. It's not safe out here."

Mike looks around once more before going back inside.

"What happened?"

Tracey looks at the kitchen floor and sees the broken glass on the floor.

"I do not know, but I am going to get to the bottom of this."

Mike proceeds to call the police as Tracey starts to clean up the broken glass on the floor. He says, "Baby, I am so sorry about this drama. You don't deserve this."

She starts to cry.

"Tracey, it is going be okay. This is not your fault."

About 30 minutes later, the police arrive and take their statements. They look around in the woods outside but don't find any clues.

"Let's just get some rest," Mike says to her.

They make their way upstairs to bed. Tracey kisses Mike.

"I love you."

Mike gives her a warm embrace as she falls asleep. Mike can't sleep, however, as he thinks about how to handle this situation.

6

"No! No!" Tracey screams in her sleep.

"Baby, I am here. It's okay. You had another nightmare."

Tracey is in a cold sweat. She looks at the time. It is 3:30 a.m.

After a moment, he says, "I have been thinking, and I am going to hire a private investigator."

"Baby, I'm scared."

"It's going to be fine. Go back to sleep."

On Saturday, Mike wakes up very early and makes his way downstairs to make some phone calls.

"Hello, yeah...well, I need a favor... can you meet me today... someone is messing with my wife...yeah, 1 o'clock is fine...thanks, man."

Tracey makes her way down stairs before the kids wake.

"Who was on the phone?"

"I made an appointment to meet with Chuck. I want to put a stop to this nonsense."

Tracey looks at her husband and says to him, "Baby, I'm so sorry to have gotten you mixed up in my nonsense. You don't deserve this."

Mike immediately places his fingers over Tracey's mouth to quiet her. "Remember these words: for better or for worse. Your hurts are mine. I love you, and you don't have to apologize for anything that happened in your past."

Mike hugs his wife and begins to get ready for the meeting. At about noon, the kids are playing in the den.

Tracey's walks in and says, "Everybody come and eat. Lunch is ready."

The kids sit at the table and say the blessing before eating their lunch.

"Honey, I will talk to you later," Mike says as he kisses Tracey.

"Bye, Daddy."

"Bye, kids. Be good for Mommy."

"Hey, Mike. Long time, no speak," says Chuck Gatling, the private eye.

"Hey Chuck. It's good to see you again."

"Hey, how is Tracey doing, man? Is she okay?"

"To be honest, she is putting up a brave front in public. She keeps waking up in cold sweats at night."

"Enough said. Let's get down to business. You two are like family to Linda and I, so I am going to handle this one personally. You have my word."

"Thanks, man. Here is the deal."

As Mike begins to explain everything to Chuck, he then begins to show him the pictures that were sent in the envelope yesterday to Tracey.

"My man, here is our first break."

He then picks up the phone and begins to talk to a friend that he knows at the post office in town.

"Hey man, it's Chuck. Who handles the run to the Jackson Estates? Cool. Do a background check for me on him," he says before ending the call. "If my hunch is right, we may have caught a break."

"Okay, I'll get out of your way, and let you do what you do best."

Chuck grabs Mike by the arm and reassures him. "Mike, I got this one. Trust me."

"I know. That's why I came to you."

About a couple hours later, the phone rings.

"Hello," Tracey answers.

"Hey, it's Chuck."

"It's good to hear your voice. I just wish it was under better circumstances."

"Don't you worry; you're like the little sister I never had."

Tracey manages a smile.

"I need to ask you some questions, if you're up for it?"

Tracey takes a seat on the couch, takes a deep breath and replies, "Shoot."

Chuck proceeds to ask her about the mailman and about the packages she received. She recounts the three visits to the best of her ability.

"That's all I need to know. Hey, we'll get him. I will call you later."

Mike then walks through the door and says, "Hey baby."

Tracey hangs up the phone, and her smile lights up the room. "That is a nice site. What's up?"

"Chuck just called. He said he's got him."

"Good ole' Chuck. He is the best. Tell you what. How about we take a vacation?" Tracey smiles at him.

He adds, "I will work out the details about where and when."

"Mike, I want Hawaii. I want to get away. I want to make love under the stars on the beach. I want my life back. I want to be fully happy again."

Later in the day, Chuck calls Mike on his cell phone.

"Hello, this is Mike."

"Mike, this is Chuck. I need to talk to you as soon as possible."

"Okay, I am on my way."

About 15 minutes later, Mike arrives at Chuck's office.

"What's the matter?" Mike says as he notices the look on Chuck's face.

"I got some information to give you, and I really don't know how to say it."

"Just give it to me."

"Okay. Tony Parker has escaped from prison."

"We know already. We got a picture in the mail from him at my daughter's daycare."

"Oh shit. Well, here is the deal. I found out that he had a mole on the inside of the jail covering for him. The person that was delivering the packages was also someone he paid off. That person is in custody now. This is how we found out what was done. He escaped from prison 3 days ago."

After a second, he continues, "It also appears that he is stalking Tracey, and it may have been him that broke into your home yesterday."

"You have got to be kidding me."

Just then, 2 police officers come into Chuck's office. They nod and say, "Hello, Mr. Cohen. My name is Inspector Jackson. I have been assigned to take the lead on this case. We are doing everything possible to find Tony Parker so that we can place him back in custody."

"I need to warn my wife."

"Mr. Cohen, I have already assigned an unmarked car to your home. He is there right now and has already checked in with us. Your wife and family are fine. Additionally, we do believe we have a lead on capturing him. I know this is an uncomfortable situation, but I am asking that you do not say anything to your wife. We don't want to make it seem like we are on to him. Can we count on you for that?"

Mike ponders and thinks about it for a minute.

"Okay, but I don't like it."

He explains, "We did learn that Mr. Parker found out where Charisse's day care is located and tried unsuccessfully to take her out of the day care, thanks to their strict rules. I showed his picture to the one of the teacher's and they were sure it was him."

"That motherfucker. I'll kill him myself if I ever get my hands on him."

"Mr. Cohen, I know what you're feeling, but we need you to calm down."

"Calm down! What the hell are you smoking? Calm down! This motherfucker went to my daughter's school and tried to kidnap her, and you want me to calm down. Are you serious? Have you ever been in my shoes before, man?"

"Actually, sir, I have been in your shoes before, and to be honest, I know exactly how you feel. I praise God for keeping my family safe. This is one of the reasons why I was assigned to handle this case."

Hearing the Inspector, he sits down in the chair and begins to calm down a little.

"Look, no disrespect intended towards you, but I need to protect my family."

"I got you on that, sir. Know that we have a plan to catch the culprit.

We just need your co-operation."

When Mike hesitates, he says, "Please, Mr. Cohen. I want to remind you to not say anything to your wife at this time."

Mike leaves the office with a purpose. He hurries back home to his wife and children who sit in the den and watch television.

"Unit one checking in. Looks like the husband just pulled up to the house," reports the undercover squad car.

Meanwhile, down the street, Tony has hired a lookout to stalk the Cohen house.

"Hey Tony. It looks like the father just pulled up. What do you want me to do?"

"Sit tight, keep your distance and let me know if anyone else shows up."

"Hi, Daddy."

The kids run to him. Mike gives the kids each a big a hug and kiss. Tracey takes a look at her husband and knows that something is bothering him.

She looks into his eyes, smiles at him and mouths the words, "What's wrong?"

Mike tries his best to fake a smile at his knowing wife, but they know each other too well for that. Tracey tells the kids to continue to watch TV as she takes him by the hand to the other room to talk.

"Baby, what's the matter? I can tell something is on your mind."

"I am okay, sweetie. I am just glad to see you is all."

Tracey looks at him again, and in a more serious voice, "Michael Cohen, don't you sit there and tell me that lie. Do not shut me out. I want to know what's going on."

Mike remembers what the police had told him, but he knew that he could not lie to his wife. "Baby, please listen to me."

Mike goes on to explain what he was told by Inspector Jackson at Chuck's office.

Tracey takes a deep breath and says to herself, "Ok, I can do this."

Mike takes Tracey's hand, "Are you okay?"

Tracey smiles at her husband, embraces him and then whispers, "As long as I am in your arms every night, I will be just fine."

Mike just smiles and says to her, "I cannot believe how calm you are."

Tracey is scared to death on the inside, but she promised herself that she wouldn't let her ex get to her mentally ever again.

Several minutes later, a car parks at the beginning of the street. Tony's lookout gets into the car.

Meanwhile, outside the Cohen house, the unmarked unit checks in with headquarters.

"This is Unit 1, I think we have some activity going on. There is a blue Sedan sitting 4 doors down from the Cohen household. 3 Males, 2 African-American and 1 Hispanic."

"Unit 1, can you make out their faces?"

"Negative, I can't get a visual. Unit 2, do a walk by."

"Roger that."

He walks past the car like a pedestrian.

When he walks down the street, he gives a thumb's down to Unit 1. "That's not him," Unit 1 says over the walkie-talkie.

"Unit 3, set up a road block at Foxwood and Jackson. Block the entrance into the subdivision."

Meanwhile, Tony is in the car on the next street over, going over the plan once more with the 2 men.

"I killed the last guy because he fucked up. Don't make me do the same to you," Tony warns them.

Miguel and Marcus just nod their heads and proceed to get out of the car.

Tony sends a text to someone and tells them to send the package. A UPS truck pulls up a couple of doors down, and a deliveryman gets out. Tony and his henchmen get out the car and proceed into the woods to take up position.

The driver knocks at the side door.

"Who is it?"

Mike comes downstairs with his gun in hand, makes his way to the garage door and comes around the back of the house cautiously.

"Package for Tracey Parker."

Mike slowly moves around the house so not to tip him off.

"Freeze!" Mike yells.

"Don't shoot."

Suddenly, two shots are fired from the woods. One hits Cheryl in the left shoulder. The other kills the delivery man. She falls to the ground, and a loud scream is heard inside the house.

"Shots fired! Shots fired! I need back up to the Cohen House stat."

"Roger that. I need all available units to proceed to 1130 Walker Place. Shots fired, undercover officers on the scene."

"Tracey!" Mike screams.

"Cheryl!" Tracey yells back.

Almost immediately, another shot is fired from the woods from a different direction. The shot hits the siding of the house. Everyone takes cover. Another shot shatters the window next to the door.

Mike yells out to everyone in the house to stay down and away from the windows. The kids are crying and screaming from further inside. Mike sneaks around a broken down car and enters the woods from behind the neighbor's house.

Mike can see Tony through his binoculars and slowly sneaks up on him. The other hit man continues to fire at the house again from another part of the woods.

Chuck, who was lying in wait, sneaks up into position and yells, "Freeze."

The hit man makes a sudden move to turn around and points his gun at Chuck to fire at him, but Chuck shoots him in the chest twice. At the same time, Mike inches up on Tony as he continues to fire repeatedly at the house. Mike is boiling mad and steps on a branch. Tony hears the branch break and immediately turns around and shoots. Mike ducks down, takes cover and returns fire. One of his rounds hits Tony in the stomach.

"Oh shit."

"Get on your hands and knees right now," Mike yells.

"Chuck, over here. I got him."

"On my way."

Chuck arrives and immediately radios for help.

"I need another bus in the woods behind 1130 Walker Place. Gunshot wound to the stomach."

A police officer runs towards the fallen gunman as he sees Tracey trying to help her fallen sister. The kids come downstairs and see the blood. They all begin to scream. Chuck comes running over.

"Are you okay, Mike?"

"Yeah, I am. Get an ambulance. My sister in law has been hit."

"Already called in."

Chuck repeats the call for the ambulance. "Central situation is all clear. I need a bus to 1130 Walker Place for a gunshot victim."

Once the ambulance arrives and pulls into the driveway, the paramedics immediately begin to stop Cheryl's bleeding. She has lost a lot of blood from the gunshot wound.

"Start an IV on her. Stat," one medic says as they lift her onto a gurney and wheel her away.

At the same time, two other paramedics push Tony towards the second ambulance.

"Take this piece of trash to the hospital," Chuck loudly says. "We should've let you die."

"What hospital are you taking her to?" Mike says.

"Brunswick Memorial Hospital, sir."

The paramedics immediately load Cheryl down the driveway and into the ambulance. Tracey immediately says a prayer for her unconscious sister, knowing that she is in bad shape. The paramedics rush Tony into a different ambulance and leave for the hospital too. Detective Parker rides with them since Tony is now in his custody.

"Stay with your family. I will call you as soon as I know something."

"Thank you, Chuck," Tracey says.

Mike shakes hands with Chuck as he leaves.

"You okay, baby?" Tracey asks him.

"I will be."

Mike calls his parents to tell them what has happened. Meanwhile, Tracey is on the phone with her parents and gives them the news about Cheryl.

After an hour, Detective Parker calls Mike and Tracey from the hospital, "Cheryl has died from the gunshot wound. The bullet nicked a vein, and she lost too much blood."

45

"No! No! That bastard killed my sister!" Tracey screams.

She cries in Mike's arms.

"Mr. Cohen, I am so sorry. Please take your time with your wife. We will take your statements later."

His parents arrive at the house and quickly make their way inside. They look at the bullet holes and the shattered glass on the floor. Mike gives them the news.

"My God," Milton says.

"Tracey, I'm so sorry for your loss. Cheryl was an amazing woman and will be missed dearly."

As they grieve together, the phone rings. Chuck is on the phone from the police station.

"Hello, yeah man...I am on my way," Mike says.

"Tracey, let's go. We need to go see Cheryl."

"You and Tracey go handle your business. We can stay with the kids," Mary says.

In 15 minutes' time, Tracey and Mike make their way to the hospital with a purpose.

"I hope he gets the death penalty for killing Cheryl."

Mike reaches for his wife's hand to comfort her as he continues to drive. As soon as they walk into the hospital, they head for the nurse's station.

"I am the sister of Cheryl Martin. I need to claim the body."

Inspector Jackson comes around the corner after talking with a few detectives about the case and sees Mike and Tracey.

"I am so sorry for your loss, Tracey."

After a moment, he continues, "Mr. Parker is in critical condition from the gunshot wound. He may not make it."

Tracey then gets a look in her eyes, and she is full of fury.

"I want to see him!" Tracey demands.

"Look, I understand how emotional you must be after everything that has happened, but I can't let you do that right now."

"I want to see him! He killed my sister with a bullet that was meant for me. I don't give a rat's ass that he may not make it through the night. I promise that I won't jump on him, although I want to, but I need closure for all the years of torture he has put me through."

"Is she serious?" the Inspector asks.

"Yes, she is, and I want to see him also."

"Okay. Let me see what I can do."

Inspector Jackson leaves for a couple of minutes and then comes back. He says to them, "I will give you 5 minutes."

"Lord, please give me the strength to do this," Tracey says after a deep breath.

Mike just squeezes her hand and nods his head in agreement. They follow the officer with a purpose. When they turn the corner, Tracey hesitates for a moment and then locks eyes with her ex-husband.

"You're the scum of the earth. I hope you get the death penalty," Tracey growls.

Mike suddenly recognizes Tony as the same person who delivered the 2nd package to the house. A sudden rage comes over him as he takes a step towards Tony. The police officer reaches out to hold him back.

Tony looks up from the hospital bed and sees his ex-wife standing there. Tony just blows a kiss at her. He musters up the strength to say, "So, this is the sucker you tried to replace me with." He then coughs.

"What's up punk? Remember me? I bet you he can't hit that ass like I can. You know I would have her squealing like the trick she is."

"You son of a bitch, you killed my sister."

Tony just smiles, "I never liked the bitch anyway, but that should have been you instead of her."

"Alright, alright," the Inspector says.

"You know what, you piece of shit," Mike yells at Tony.

Mike tries to get at him, but the officers are holding him back.

"Mike, come on. Lets go," Tracey says. "This scum isn't worth being in my presence."

"You won't have to worry about him again," Inspector Jackson says to them. "If he survives, they are looking at capital charges against him: 1st degree murder."

"My sister... I have lost my best friend."

As Mike and Tracey take one final look at Tony handcuffed to the bed, tears begin to form in Tracey's eye.

"You better die. If you don't, you'll wish you were dead."

They walk to the waiting room and find Tracey's mom and dad. Tracey's mom begins to cry as she hugs Tracey tightly.

Todd embraces his son in law and tells him, "Thank you for being there for my daughter throughout all of this."

As Mike and Tracey make their way home, Tracey begins to think about the many nightmares, the flashbacks, the beatings and the abuse. Then, she starts to cry when Cheryl's smiling face comes to her mind.

7

3 Months Later

I think we need a vacation to get away from all of this craziness."

"Oh, Michael. I would love that. Do you have the vacation time? I have two weeks left."

"Do you want to go to Hawaii or Mexico?"

Tracey gasps, "Hawaii! Oh, Mike. Can we afford it? Are we taking the kids, or will it be just us?"

"Yes, I believe we can."

"Let's make it a family affair."

They hug and proceed to go to bed.

"Mike, I know I told you this earlier, but thank you for being there for me."

"Baby, you don't have to thank me for that. We are one."

"When can we leave, baby?"

"How does 3 weeks sound? Is that enough time for you to get a week off? The kids are out of school then."

"Baby, I cannot wait. I love you so much."

She hugs him and kisses him good night.

The next day, Mike wakes Tracey up with a soft kiss and breakfast in bed.

"Baby, what time is it? Did I oversleep?"

"No, honey. I just got up early to make you breakfast. The kids are already eating."

"Oh okay. Thank you, baby."

Mike continues to get the kids clothes out for church.

"Daddy, can I wear my blue dress?" Charisse says.

"Yes, you can wear that."

"Good morning, my baby girl. How is Mommy's little girl doing today?"

"I am okay, Mommy."

"Hi, Mom," Jason says.

Both kids give her a hug.

"Hey, Mommy," Ashley says as she runs to hug her.

"Hello, Mommy," Jason says as he comes to hug her also.

"Mom, is everything really over with him?" Jason asks.

Tracey holds him and replies, "Yes, Son, it really is. He won't bother us anymore."

"Everyone get dressed. We don't want to be late," Mike says.

The family heads to church and goes out to lunch after service. After dinner, the kids change their clothes and go outside to play. Tracey checks in on them ever so often. Mike goes into the den to watch the game on the television.

"Who's playing, honey?"

"Detroit and New York."

Tracey sits down next to her husband and starts watching the game with him. This is one of the few days where neither of them has any deadlines or demands on their time. Sunday is always a relaxing family day, where they can just relax and be themselves. About an hour later, the phone rings. Tracey's friend Chante calls.

"Hey girl," Tracey says.

"Hey, Tracey. How are you feeling?"

"Much better now, thanks. I am just trying to unwind. This has been one crazy week."

"Hey. Ray and I want to know if you guys feel like playing some cards later."

"Let me check with Mike."

Overhearing the conversation, he nods.

"Mike said bring it on."

"Oh really? See you about six, okay?"

"See you then."

Six o'clock comes around, and Ray and Chante come over. They play cards for a couple of hours and go home. Mike and Tracey begin to start looking at brochures for Hawaii.

"Baby, what about this package? It looks interesting," Mike says.

"Honey, I know we said we would take the kids, but I want to do this alone—just the two of us. What do you think?"

"I love it, baby."

We can plan another trip with the kids," Tracey replies.

4 weeks pass by, and Mike and Tracey are on a 12-hour flight to Hawaii. The plane lands, and they get their bags. They then proceed to the hotel they booked.

Mike smiles at Tracey and says, "This looks familiar."

Tracey lets out a big laugh at the check in and proceeds to their room. Their room is on the first floor, and the back door opens to the beach.

"Oh, Mike. Look at the scenery."

Mike comes up behind Tracey and just holds her as they look at the sunset.

"Baby, let's walk the beach in the moonlight."

"Okay. Let me get a towel in case we get a little tired."

They see the boardwalk as Mike points to her to go in that direction. As they walk along, they hear the sound of the waves pounding the shore.

"Tracey, are you sure you're okay after everything?"

Tracey stops and looks at Mike.

"Mike, I don't think I will ever be able to fully be able to thank you for what you have done for me. Some men might have just walked out on a wife under those circumstances. I love you. I thank God for you each day. I am slowly but surely getting over that fiasco."

She stands on her toes to give him a peck on the lips. They walk on the shore in matching short outfits while holding hands together. Mike stops for a second to look at the waves hitting the sand. Tracey begins to smile as she holds onto her husband. Mike begins to kiss her as she begins to caress his body. Mike takes the towel and lays it out on the beach. They began to kiss and cuddle while the moon provides the only light. The sound of the waves hitting the shore mixes with the sounds of love making coming from Mike and Tracey.

8

After six months of Tony's lawyers making motions on his upcoming trial, the opening statements are finally set to begin.

The prosecutor, Mr. James Lucas, stands up from his seat and walks towards the jury. He stands there for a second and takes a deep breath.

"Ladies and gentlemen of the jury, the State of New York will prove to you beyond a shadow of a doubt that the defendant, Anthony Derrick Parker, is guilty on all counts of the charges he is facing. We will show how he broke out of prison, stalked his ex-wife, fired a deadly weapon into a home, attempted to murder his ex-wife, and ultimately killed his ex-sister-in-law. Some of the evidence that you will see before you will be graphic in nature, but it will show the length that the defendant was willing to go to harass and try and stalk his ex-wife. It is your duty to find him guilty on all charges, so that we can give this family closure and make sure the defendant will never be able to harm this family or the people of New York again. Thank you."

He finishes his opening statement and proceeds back to his seat. The defense counsel, Mrs. Gloria Robinson, stands up and walks towards the jury box.

"Ladies and gentlemen of the jury, the prosecution will try and say that my client did all the outrageous things that he is charged with. We will prove that they are exaggerating the charges. He should be found not guilty on all charges. Thank you."

Tracey is ready to explode after she hears the opening remarks of the defense counsel, but Mike holds her hand and whispers in her ear, "Everything is going to be okay."

"Call your first witness, Mr. Lucas," says the judge.

"The people call Correction Officer John Abrams to the stand."

He is sworn in and then sits down.

"Officer Abrams, please tell the court where your place of employment is?"

"I work for the New York State Department of Corrections. I am assigned to the Montauk County Maximum Correction Center."

"Was the defendant assigned to your cell block?"

"Yes, he was."

"When you did your morning rounds on Wednesday, April 9th, what did you notice?"

"I walked my normal routine preparing for morning roll call, and we noticed the cell of the defendant was opened. His bed was made up to make you think someone was sleeping in it. Upon further investigation, we noticed 2 bricks loose behind the cot. It led to the exhaust system."

"What did you do next?"

"We immediately placed everyone back in their cells and did a full manhunt. I reported my findings to my superior officer."

"No further questions. Your witness."

"How old is the Montauk County Jail?"

"I have no idea."

"Isn't it over 50 years old?"

"I guess."

"How often do you check for loose bricks?"

"We normally don't check for loose bricks."

"Well, if you normally don't check for bricks, then how can you be so sure that my client loosened those bricks and escaped through them?"

When the officer doesn't answer, the defense states, "No further questions."

Mr. Lucas says, "The people call Detective Parker to the stand."

"Detective Parker, on the morning of April 9th, were you summoned to the Montauk County Jail?"

"Yes, I was."

"Please tell us about your investigation."

"Well, we examined the cell and checked the exhaust system. We found out that he had a correction officer helping him on the inside."

"Objection! Assumes facts not in evidence."

"Sustained."

"No further questions."

Defense counsel makes his way to the witness box.

"When was the last time you did a sweep on my client's cell?"

"We sweep a cell daily and on suspicion of contraband."

"Did you sweep my client's cell on the night before his alleged breakout?"

"Yes, we did."

"What did you find?"

"His cell was clean."

"No further questions."

Tracey knows what comes next.

"The people call Michael Cohen to the stand."

Mike pecks Tracey on the lips, stands and walks towards the witness box. Tony locks eyes with Mike and quietly mouths the word, "Bitch ass punk."

Mike mouths back to him, "I will fuck you up if you make it out of here."

"Mr. Cohen, please tell me about the incident of the object being thrown through the window of your home."

"Well, at about 7:30 p.m., my family was at home, and a brick was thrown through our front window. It scared my wife and children. I ran downstairs with my registered handgun and proceeded outside to see if the people who did it were still there, but the cowards left."

"What else happened?"

"Anonymous packages and letters were being sent to the house containing pictures, including one of the idiot at the defendant's table standing in front of my step daughter."

"Objection to the name characterization of my client."

"Sustained. Please try to control yourself, sir."

"Yes, sir."

"Another package was delivered the next day, and that's when shots were fired from the woods next to my home. One of the shots killed my sister-in-law, though they were meant for my wife."

"Objection, assumes facts not in evidence."

"Sustained."

"I went out the side door, went through the back woods of my house, and proceeded toward where the shots were being fired from. I encountered the defendant, and when he saw me, he took a shot at me. I returned fire and struck him in the stomach."

"Thank you. Nothing further."

The defense makes his way to the witness.

"So, is it your testimony that you intentionally shot my client in the stomach?"

"After he shot my sister in law and took a shot at me, yes."

"Move to strike the last statement as non-responsive."

"Over ruled."

"Mr. Cohen, is it a fact that you are so jealous of my client that you intentionally made up this story and shot my client on purpose?"

"No, your client was trespassing on my property, shooting at my house and family, and shooting at me."

"Aren't you just making up this entire story to get sympathy for your wife?"

"Look, your client is a piece of trash, and his actions have landed him in this position. Your client is going to get what he has coming to him, one way or another."

"Are you making a threat against my client?"

Mike just smiles and says, "I am not threatening your client."

The lawyer looks at Mike for a couple of minutes and turns his back.

"No further questions."

After a moment, the prosecutor says, "The people call Tracey Cohen to the stand."

Tracey makes her way to the witness stand. She looks over at Tony, who sits at the witness table. He blows her a kiss. She rolls her eyes and places her hand on the Bible to be sworn in.

As she sits down, her ex-mother-in-law walks into the courtroom, almost on cue. Tracey locks eyes on Debra Parker and takes a deep breath. Mike notices the sudden change in her demeanor, turns around and notices the woman coming down the aisle who takes a seat in the front row behind Tony. Her eyes are fixed, and her attitude is cold as she looks directly at Tracey.

"Mrs. Cohen, please tell the court about your relationship with the defendant."

"He is my ex-husband."

"Can you tell me who is in this picture?"

"My ex-husband took a selfie with our daughter at the daycare my sister ran before he murdered her."

"Objection."

"Sustained. Mrs. Cohen, please just answer the questions asked of you."

Tracey nods her head to the judge.

"Mrs. Cohen, did your ex-husband have visitation rights to see your daughter?"

"No, the son of a bitch was supposed to be locked up in jail."

"Your Honor, I object!"

"Sustained. Control yourself, Mrs. Cohen. This is your last warning."

"Who sent the pictures to you?"

"The pictures were sent to me anonymously. There was no return address."

"Did your ex-husband send you these pictures?"

"We believed that he was behind it. We contacted a private investigator. That's when we found out that he escaped from prison."

"Objection, assumes facts not in evidence."

"Sustained. Counsel approach the bench."

The prosecution and defense counsel make their way up to the judge.

"Mr. Lucas, if you can't control your witness, I am going to declare a mistrial. Am I understood?"

"Yes, Your Honor."

Both attorneys make their way back to their respective tables.

"Let's break for lunch. That will give time for cooler heads to prevail. Court is adjourned."

During the lunch break, Debra walks up to Tracey and Mike.

"We need to talk."

"Look Debra, I have nothing to say to you. You better leave me the hell alone."

"Lady, I don't know who you are, but you need to back up off my wife."

"Who is this bitch ass sucker for a man? Look ass wipe, you need to mind your business before I open up a can on your ass."

"Look, lady. I am trying to be polite."

Just then a court officer walks over.

"Is there a problem here?"

"No, just family catching up, Officer," Debra says with a fake smile.

Debra whispers loud enough for Tracey to hear her, "I will fuck you up."

"Bitch, please," Tracey whispers back and looks at her with a side eye.

Debra turns around and walks off. She motions to another woman to meet her outside.

After lunch, the parties return to the courtroom, and the court officer steps forward to bring the court to attention.

"All rise!"

"Be seated," the judge responds and sits down. "Mr. Lucas, please continue with your direct examination of your witness."

"Thank you, Your Honor. Mrs. Cohen, what was the verdict that was given to your ex-husband at his previous trial three years ago?"

"He was given a sentence of 20 years."

"Were you notified that his sentence had been vacated?"

"No."

"What happened at your house seven months ago?"

"It first started with packages being delivered anonymously. Then, a rock was thrown through the window. Finally, my back doorbell rang, and my sister answered the door."

She takes a deep breath and tries to fight back tears from forming.

"My twin sister was murdered when she answered the door. The shot came from the woods on the side of my house."

When she says that, a smirk begins to form on Tony's face.

"No further questions."

"Your Honor, I would like to reserve my cross examination of this witness at a later date."

"So ordered. You are still under oath, but you are not to discuss any part of your testimony with anyone."

Tracey steps down from the witness stand with a puzzled look on her face. She keeps her focus and sits next to her husband.

After a few more witnesses from the police and investigators, the prosecution begins to shape its case and rests.

"Mrs. Robinson, please call your first witness."

"The defense calls Tony Parker to the stand."

Tony stands up from the defense table and makes his way to the witness box to be sworn in.

"Do you swear to tell the truth, the whole truth and nothing but the truth so help you God?"

"I do."

"State your name for the record."

"My name is Anthony Derrick Parker."

"Mr. Parker, did you break out of prison?"

"No, I didn't. I was released pending a new trial."

Tony's attorney, Ms. Robinson, interjects, "Your Honor, I have documents that prove that my client did not break out of jail as the prosecution alleges."

"Your Honor," retorts Mr. Lucas, "the state doesn't know anything about this documentation, and we question its legitimacy. In addition, we have not been notified of a ruling that released the defendant from custody."

"I am providing the state with a federal order that released my client from custody."

The prosecution takes a look at the documentation provided to him and immediately asks to approach the bench.

"Your Honor, these documents that the defense has just provided us look suspect to say the least. There is no raised seal, and a couple of words are misspelled. I ask that we be allowed to check the validity of these documents with the issuing judge."

"Prosecution motion is denied. The documents look valid on its face."

"Your Honor."

"Don't push it, counselor. Now, step back, and let's get on with this trial before I hold you in contempt."

As the prosecution walks back to their table, he leans over to his assistant and says, " Go search court records and see if there is a prior relationship between the defense counsel and the judge. Something smells fishy."

"Proceed, Mrs. Robinson."

"Mr. Parker, did you stalk and send packages to the home of your ex-wife?"

"No, ma'am, I didn't. I don't know where they got that idea from."

"Then, how do you explain the picture sent of you and your daughter at the daycare?"

"Simple, someone stole my cell phone, printed up the picture and sent it to her. I haven't seen my little girl since she was a baby. I wanted to see her."

"Mr. Parker, can you please tell the court what happened 7 months ago?"

As he begins to speak, a disturbance starts up on the side of the courtroom, and at the same time, someone stands up in the back of the courtroom, runs up to the front, and fires two shots at Tony. Panic and hysteria break out all over. The court officers immediately shoot the gunman as Tony clutches his chest where he has been shot. He then leans towards over the banister to the witness box and falls to the ground.

Debra Parker yells, "Tony!" and rushes to his fallen body.

"Remove the jury, and clear the courtroom now!"

"Call an ambulance!"

Mike immediately covers Tracey as the court officers take control of the situation. Mike peeks up over the banister and helps Tracey up as they both look at Tony's lame body on the courtroom floor.

Tracey begins to realize what has happened, and she takes Mike's hand and holds onto it tightly.

"Mr. and Mrs. Cohen, we need to take your statements of what you witnessed."

The police question everyone in the courtroom. The EMS workers immediately rush Tony and the shooter's body out of the courtroom.

Debra immediately follows.

She takes one step at Tracey and says, "I will fuck you up."

"I hope he dies. I wish it was you, bitch," Tracey yells back. She clutches Mike's hand as it still shakes.

Debra takes another step towards Tracey but then turns to catch up with the EMS workers and her son. She climbs into the ambulance and then takes out her phone.

She sends a group text and types, "Tony was killed today. Find out who did it!"

She then sends out another text to a different contact and tells them, "Plan B goes into effect now. Tony was murdered. Wait for further instructions when I get confirmation on the target."

9

One Week Later

Debra drives to the office of Inspector Jackson.

"I want to know what happened to my son, and you never called to tell me the progress."

"Ms. Parker, I apologize for the murder of your son, but at this time, we have no leads on what happened or who was responsible. As soon as I have some information, you will be the first to know."

"Son of a bitch," she mumbles to herself. "You haven't done a damn thing to solve this case, but don't worry. I have my own ways. You're probably in on it," Debra yells as she leaves the police station.

"What a waste of a woman," another officer says as he walks towards Jackson's office.

"You okay, boss?"

"Yeah, I'm good. Excuse me, I need to make a call."

After a moment, he says, "Hello, Mrs. Cohen. This is Inspector Jackson. I am calling to let you know the case involving the murder of Tony Parker has been closed. We don't have any information on the person who killed him."

An hour later, a card comes in the mail. Tracey opens the card and reads: "Tracey, now that he is dead, you can close that horrific chapter of your life."

She looks at the card and just smiles as she places it back in the envelope, proceeds to light the card and place it in the fireplace. The card burns slowly as Tracey smiles, sits back in her recliner chair and sips the glass of wine she was drinking earlier.

"Yes, he is," she mumbles under her breath.

Tracey has finally received a second chance.